The Best Pet

An Animal Friends Reader

by Liza Charlesworth
illustrated by Ian Smith

ISBN: 978-0-545-85961-5

10 17 18 19/0

Printed in the U.S.A. 40
First printing 2015

Book design by Maria Mercado

SCHOLASTIC INC.

A dog is the best pet.

DOG

A cat is the best pet.

A fish is the best pet.

A bird is the best pet.

A turtle is the best pet.

A snake is the best pet.

A rabbit is the best pet.

A hamster is the best pet.

A lizard is the best pet.

An elephant is the best pet.

No!

Comprehension Boosters

1. Find the animal eating carrots. What animal do you see? Describe it.

2. Why isn't an elephant a good pet?

3. What pet do you think is best? Why?